V

20 1

CREEPY-CRAWLY
STORIES

GW00729205

CREEPY-CRAWLY
STORIES

Compiled by Barbara Ireson

Illustrated by Lesley Smith

BEAVER BOOKS

A Beaver Book

Published by Arrow Books Limited
62–65 Chandos Place, London WC2N 4NW

An imprint of Century Hutchinson Ltd

London Melbourne Sydney Auckland
Johannesburg and agencies throughout the world

First published by Hutchinson Children's Books 1986
Beaver edition 1987
Text © Century Hutchinson 1986
Illustrations © Lesley Smith 1986

Made and printed in Great Britain
by Anchor Brendon Ltd
Tiptree, Essex

ISBN 0 09 951230 0

Contents

The Insect Kingdom that didn't get started
Margaret Mahy   7

Aunt Emily's Pangolin
Howard Hoy   12

The Fly who had Christmas Dinner
Ann North   19

Grottie Germ and his Relations
Elaine   23

Lizard comes down from the North
Anita Hewett   25

Reginald's Lousy Adventure
Sarah Morcom   32

The Spider and the Prince
Mies Bouhuys   37

The Elephant and the Beetle
Patricia Adams   43

The Big Sore Toe
Joanne Horniman   46

Dribble's House
Mies Bouhuys   50

Mr Learn-a-lot and the Singing Midges
Alf Prøysen   56

Spider's Surprise
Sarah Morcom   62

Big Spider gets a Fright
Elizabeth Robinson   69

Tumf
W. J. Corbett   73

Little Fly on the Ceiling
Angela Pickering   78

Wriggly Worm and the Evil Weevil
Eugenie Summerfield   82

The Box
Marion Spring   87

Sock Eater
Jean Chapman   91

The Insect Kingdom that didn't get started

Margaret Mahy

There are seven hundred thousand different sorts of insects, and once there was very nearly a wonderful insect kingdom full of insects who understood one another and were loving and kind. It happened like this.

A spider caught a fly in her web and was just going to wrap him up like a school lunch when a woman vacuuming sucked the spider, the fly, the cobweb and all, into the vacuum cleaner.

The spider pulled her legs in tight so as not to lose any. She was whirled round and round down a long black tunnel until at last she reached a place where all was dark and soft and dusty. There was a roaring noise in the air, but the whirling had stopped. The spider looked with all her eight eyes, but she could not see a single thing. She couldn't think what had happened.

At last the woman switched off the vacuum cleaner and all was quiet.

'Help!' the spider called. 'Help! Help!'

'Who's that calling "Help"?' asked a voice almost in her ear.

'It's me, a poor spider,' the spider replied. 'Who is there?'

'Oh, it's you, spider baby,' said the voice. 'I'm a fly you were going to eat, just a few minutes ago. We're both in this thing together.'

'Oh!' cried the spider. 'Am I glad to hear you! What's happened, do you suppose? Is it the end of the world?'

'Heck no!' said the fly carelessly. 'We've just been eaten by something bigger than both of us. That's the way things are. Spiders eat flies, birds eat spiders, cats eat birds. It's either eat or get eaten in this life.'

The spider was silent for a while.

'I didn't think it would end like this,' she said at last. 'Now I feel sorry for all the flies I've eaten in the past. If only I could get out of here I'd live my life differently, I can tell you.'

'Funny you should say that,' said the fly. 'I was thinking the same thing. If only I could have my time over again, I'd be a different fly. I'd stay away from rubbish heaps and I'd never walk all over someone's meat with dirty shoes on again.'

'I'd learn to eat berries,' the spider declared. 'I'd drink honey like a butterfly. I'm not really an insect myself, but I'd learn insect ways.'

'Come to think, spider baby,' the fly said. 'I don't suppose a fly and a spider ever had a chance to understand each other's point of view before. We've never had the chance to talk together as we're talking now.'

'And to think the chance should have come too late,' the spider wept. 'Why, if we'd known then what we know now, we could have changed the world.'

8

And they went on talking together in the smothering darkness of the vacuum cleaner bag, dreaming of what might have been, sobbing and moaning, 'Too late! Too late!' and 'If only we had a second chance.' They dreamed of a wonderful kingdom where spiders and insects understood each other and were loving and kind. Then the woman came back from her lunch and emptied the bag of dust on to the compost heap.

'This is it!' cried the fly as they were taken and shaken up and down. 'This is it, spider baby.' Dust, pieces of paper, breadcrumbs, scraps of orange peel, pins, threads and fluff swelled and swirled pellmell, holus bolus around them.

'Too late, dear fly, too late,' the spider replied faintly.

But it wasn't too late! When the spider recovered from her faint she found herself bruised, but otherwise well and strong, on the compost heap. She stretched her legs. They were all there. She set to work and made a new web. Just as she finished it she saw a fly sitting on a leaf, cleaning his wings with his hind legs and watching her.

'Is that you, dear fly?' she asked hopefully.

'Is that you, spider baby?' replied the fly.

'I've just finished making the prettiest web,' the spider went on. 'It's a new sort of peaceful web. Come and see it.'

'It looks a lot like the last one,' the fly replied. 'I think I'll stay here.'

'But fly – we're friends now,' the spider pleaded. 'All the wicked past is forgotten. Don't you remember our plans, our dreams?'

'I haven't forgotten,' the fly replied. 'But it doesn't

seem as important now as it did then. I mean, like, it was dark and dusty then, and it's bright and sunny now. And I am a fly and, after all, spider baby, you *are* a spider. I'm off.'

'Where are you going?' shrieked the spider.

'Off to find a good dirty rubbish heap, and then to walk all over someone's lunch in my dirty boots,' the fly replied and he flew away.

The spider hung herself head downwards in the exact centre of her new web.

'It's terrible the way some people forget their dreams of better things. There are not many people prepared to struggle for a better world. And he was so fat and delicious looking too. Never mind. There'll be another one along soon.'

And that is how the kingdom of the insects didn't get started after all. Aren't we lucky, you and I, that we would have more sense than that.

Aunt Emily's Pangolin

Howard Hoy

Mr Francis sat in a deck chair, under the shade of his favourite peach tree. It was a very hot summer's day. Above the tall banks of flowers, which stood all around the garden, big striped bees hovered and tortoiseshell butterflies danced in the fresh breeze.

Mr Francis was reading a letter which he had received that morning from his Aunt Emily who lived in Africa. Like Aunt Emily, the letter was short, sweet and rather mysterious: *Dear Henry. Arriving soon. Looking forward to seeing you. Love Aunt Emily.*

Mr Francis scratched his head in surprise and turned the letter over to look at the stamp. As he did so, something black and wriggling fell into his hand. Mr Francis peered through his spectacles and saw a large, black ant. He frowned and looked up into the branches above his head. He was just in time to see the last of a long column of ants disappearing into the green foliage. Very carefully he picked a leaf and looked at it. Then he gasped with horror, for the leaf was curling at the edges.

'Oh dear, oh dear,' said Mr Francis as he pulled off another dying leaf and another black ant hurried along

12

the branch past his fingers. 'These wretched ants are killing my tree. I will have to do something immediately.'

Mr Francis ran across his garden and looked over the wooden fence which divided him from Miss Ida Sparkle, but she wasn't there. So he ran back across the garden and looked over the fence which separated him from Mr Alfred Grubbage.

Mr Grubbage was standing in the middle of his small, rather yellow lawn, practising a new golfing shot.

'Mr Grubbage,' called Mr Francis anxiously. 'Could you spare me one minute please?'

Mr Grubbage sliced his shot and then looked around.

'Oh, it's you is it, Mr Francis?'

'Yes, Mr Grubbage. I wondered if you could help me.'

Mr Grubbage scratched the hair under his golfing cap. 'Now that depends on what it is.'

'It's ants, Mr Grubbage, they are attacking my peach tree. The one which won the fruit prize at the Horti-cultural Show.'

Mr Grubbage frowned. 'Nasty things are ants.' Mr Grubbage went into his garden shed and brought out a big, green bottle. 'If I were you I'd use this bottle of insecticide. It says that it gets rid of all known things.'

Mr Francis took the bottle and poured the contents very carefully all over the base of the peach tree and into the long grass which surrounded it.

'That should do the trick,' said Mr Grubbage leaning over the garden fence. 'That will fix them. You'll see, the ants will all have gone by tomorrow morning.'

The next morning Mr Francis got up very early and

13

went out into the garden to inspect his peach tree. The ants were still there, climbing steadily up and down the tree in long, black columns. The only thing which *was* different was that all the grass around the tree, where Mr Francis had poured the contents of Mr Grubbage's bottle, had become yellow and very sickly looking. He fancied the tree looked a little worse.

Later that morning, Mr Francis saw Miss Ida Sparkle coming down her garden pathway to light a bonfire.

'Miss Sparkle,' called Mr Francis, 'have you got a minute, please?' After a while, Miss Sparkle, who was a little deaf, noticed him and, putting down the bundles of newspapers which she was carrying, leant over the fence. When Mr Francis told her about the ants and the bottle which Mr Grubbage had given him Miss Ida Sparkle just chuckled. 'No use using any of old

Grubbage's remedies, Mr Francis. Get a big spade and a kettle of hot water and dig all around the tree. You'll soon find the ants' nest. Ants don't like hot baths. You take my word for it, Mr Francis.'

So Mr Francis dug all around the roots of the tree but he couldn't find the ants' nest and the ants continued to climb the tree. Up and down, down and up, all day long in twos and threes, threes and fours, fives and sixes.

Mr Francis looked back and down the garden.

All around the base of the peach tree were small, untidy piles of earth. 'And the ants are still there,' sighed Mr Francis.

The next morning, while Mr Francis was still in bed, there was a loud knock on the front door. He sprang out of bed, pulled his dressing gown over his pyjamas, and ran downstairs and opened the door. Standing there, surrounded by a huge mountain of trunks, cases and boxes, was the short, round figure of his Aunt Emily. Mr Francis's mouth fell wide open in astonishment.

'You got my letter, didn't you, Henry?' said Aunt Emily, leaning forward to give her nephew a large kiss on the cheek.

'Yes, Aunt.'

'Well, that's good, dear. One should never arrive unannounced. It is very bad manners, you know.' Aunt Emily took off the great rose-covered hat which she was wearing and tossed it on to a coat hook. 'And now, Henry, what I want is a large cup of tea, if you please.'

After they had both had breakfast, Mr Francis took his aunt out into the garden and showed her the peach tree and the withered leaves and the ants climbing up and down the tree.

'You call those ants, my dear!' exclaimed Aunt Emily incredulously. 'In Africa, we have ants that are ten times as big.' Mr Francis's eyes opened wide and he shivered slightly.

'Ten times as big, Aunt?'

'Oh yes, dear, twenty times as big in some parts, I shouldn't wonder.' Mr Francis told her how he had used the bottle of insecticide which Mr Grubbage had given him, and how Miss Sparkle had told him to dig for the nest. And he told her how it had all gone wrong and how sad he felt at the thought that his peach tree might die. His aunt listened very carefully.

'Now don't you worry, Henry,' she said. 'I have got a plan, but first I must make a telephone call.' Which she did, straight away. When she came back she said, 'Now, Henry, let us sow some new grass and fill up those silly holes you've dug.'

Just as it was growing dark, there was a loud knock on the front door. When Mr Francis opened it, he found a man holding a large box marked 'Fragile. This way up.' Mr Francis carried the box into the dining room where his aunt was sitting. It was very heavy. 'The man said that the box is for you,' said Mr Francis.

'Yes, my dear,' replied his aunt. 'I have been expecting it ever since I telephoned this morning. It will help to get rid of your ants.'

Mr Francis scratched his chin. He couldn't see how a box could help him.

Mr Francis and Aunt Emily carried the large box down the garden. They put the box carefully on the ground and Aunt Emily unfastened the catch.

'Come on, Percy,' she called loudly. 'Wake up dear.'

16

A few moments later there was the sound of a great yawn, and out of the box waddled the strangest creature. It had shiny scales and a long, waving snout.

'Whatever is it, Aunt?' asked Mr Francis.

'That, my dear, is an African pangolin. He's a pet of mine. I was going to board him at the zoo but he'll be happier with me here. He'll eat up all your ants for you, just wait and see. Tomorrow morning there won't be an ant left.'

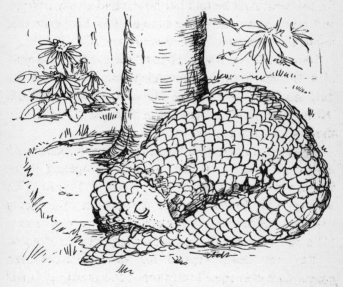

And she was absolutely right. The next morning when they went out into the garden they found that all the ants had vanished. They found Percy, too, fast asleep under the tree.

'It's hard work being an anteater,' explained Aunt Emily as they carried the sleeping creature indoors.

When Mr Grubbage and Miss Ida Sparkle heard

about the pangolin, they also wanted to borrow it to get rid of the insects and ants in *their* gardens. Soon Percy had eaten all the insects and ants in the street.

'However are we going to feed Percy now?' said Mr Francis to his aunt as Percy began shuffling around in his cage, impatient for his next meal.

'Don't worry, my dear. Your Auntie Emily will think of something.' And she did. The next morning a large notice went up outside Mr Francis's gate, and an advertisement appeared in the local newspaper. *Gardeners, stop worrying about insects this summer. Hire Percy the Pangolin to rid you of your ants.*

After that, Percy was kept very busy, but he didn't seem to mind at all. Neither did Aunt Emily. As for Mr Francis, he couldn't have been happier because his favourite peach tree was safe.

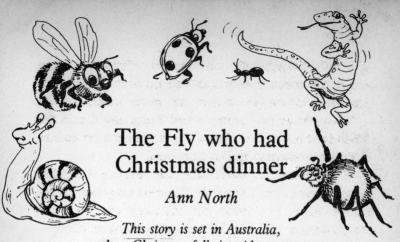

The Fly who had Christmas dinner

Ann North

*This story is set in Australia,
where Christmas falls in mid summer.*

Flo Fly, a young blowfly, was sitting on a leaf cleaning her wings. It was a hot, hot day and she could smell a wonderful food smell. What was it? Flo wanted to ask her mum, but she wasn't there. She was next door eating the cat's dinner.

Flo Fly flew off to find the wonderful smell for herself. *Bzzzzzzzzz*. Not the compost heap. *B-z-z-z-z-z-z-zzz*. What about the kitchen? M-m-mmm. That's where it was.

A man was putting a big fat turkey in the oven, and on the top of the stove saucepans were bubbling with good smells. What was happening?

Flo flitted into the next room. *B-z-z-zzzzz*. A big tree in one corner sparkled with coloured lights and shining balls. On the floor two children and two women were playing with toys. All around them were bits of coloured paper. It was very strange.

Flo flew back to the garden and found her mum sitting on the rubbish bin. 'What's happening inside that house?' Flo asked.

'It's Christmas,' said her mum.

19

'What's Christmas?'

'Christmas is wrapping things up in lots of coloured paper and people with funny hats on their heads making loud noises by pulling bits of paper apart – crackers they call them. It's all very silly, except for one thing – people eat Christmas dinner. That's the best part. They eat all sorts of nice things like turkey and roast vegetables and plum pudding with ice cream. Mmmmm!'

'Let's go,' said Flo Fly. 'I want Christmas dinner.'

'No!' said her mum.

'Why not?'

'It's dangerous. People don't like flies,' said Flo's mum.

'Why not?'

'I don't know, dear.'

'What do they do?' asked Flo.

'They chase us with a fly swat or a can of fly spray. Don't go near them, Flo! It's *dangerous*,' said her mum and flew off.

Flo sat outside in the hot sun and the wonderful smells grew stronger and more beautiful. '*Sniff . . . sniff . . .* I want Christmas dinner,' said the greedy little fly as she fluttered off towards those lovely smells. *Bzzzzzzzzzzzzzzzz*.

The family were finishing their Christmas dinner. Grandpa looked hot in the face and Daddy was being cross with the children. 'Eat your Christmas pudding at once,' he was saying. One grandma person was asleep in her chair and the other one was fanning herself with a newspaper. On the table there were dirty plates and glasses and a lot of lovely Christmas dinner leftovers.

Flo headed straight for the turkey bones. *Bzzzzzzz*.
'Get that fly!' a grandma yelled.

One of the children grabbed a fly swat and *whack* it smacked down on the table, just missing Flo.

Zizz-zizz-zizz . . . she flew up into the air and buzzed round and round the room. What could she do? Where could she go? She was very frightened.

Everyone stood up and jumped around trying to catch her.

The man grabbed a rolled-up newspaper and chased her with it. *Swipe!* It just missed her.

Faster and faster she flew. Everyone shouted and leaped at her with fly swats and rolled-up newspapers. Shout! *Whack!* Shout! *Whack! Swipe!*

Flo felt dizzy. Faster and faster, she flew around the room trying to find the way out. Suddenly there was the door. Flo zipped out into the open air and was safe.

'Silly girl, what were you doing?' asked her mother who had been buzzing in the doorway.

'I just wanted some Christmas dinner,' whimpered Flo.

'I told you not to go in there! *Zzz-zzz!* Poor dear! Why didn't you wait? I'll show you how to get your Christmas dinner – just follow me.'

Bzzzzzzzzz. She flew over to the rubbish bin and there was Grandpa scraping the leftovers from Christmas dinner into the bin. In went turkey bones, bits of vegetables, sweet sauce and big bits of Christmas pudding and melted ice cream. He put the lid on and walked off, but the bin was too full for the lid to fit properly.

Flo and her mum *zzz*-ed in and ate and ate – a yummy, wonderful Christmas dinner.

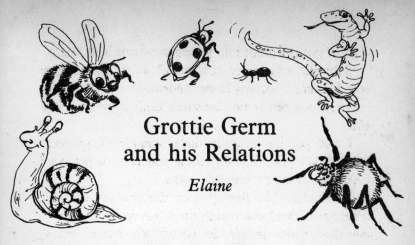

Grottie Germ
and his Relations

Elaine

Grottie Germ lived in a tooth cavity.

His mother and father lived there too.

After twenty minutes, his two brothers lived there.

After forty minutes, his four sisters lived there.

After sixty minutes (that's one hour), his eight cousins lived there.

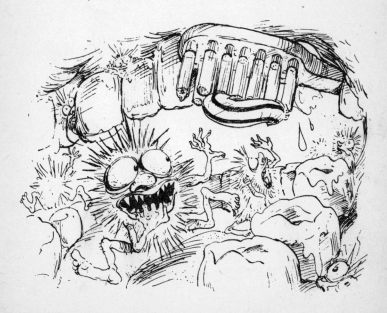

After eighty minutes his sixteen nephews lived there.

After one hundred minutes, his thirty-two nieces lived there. After one hundred and twenty minutes (that's two hours), there were sixty-four of Grottie's relations all pushing and shoving and saying,

'Move over!'

'Get off my toe!'

'Mum, his elbow is in my eye!'

'I haven't got any room!'

After one hundred and twenty-five minutes (that's two hours and five minutes), along came a toothbrush and toothpaste and washed them all down the drain.

Lizard comes down
from the North

Anita Hewett

'Happy days!' said little green Lizard, flicking his tiny tail in the air. 'I'm going to the forest. Oh, happy days!'

And he pattered along on his stumpy legs.

'It's a long, long journey I'm making,' he said. 'Over bushland and sand and grassland and scrub.'

And he hopped in the air with a squeak of delight because he felt gay and brave and adventurous.

Then Lizard looked up against the sun, and far above him the black-feathered swan beat his wings in the air, and called: 'Why are you coming down from the north, you strange little thing with a scaly back?'

But Lizard heard only the beat of strong wings as Swan flew away. So on he pattered.

Black Swan came to the sandy desert.

'I mustn't fly over the sand,' he said, and he called to Kangaroo Mouse below: 'Mouse-with-a-pocket, take my message. Go to the forest and tell them there that a creature is coming down from the north. He has scales on his back, and a flicking tail, and he's walking along on his sturdy legs.'

Mouse jumped away towards the forest. Faster and

faster and faster she raced, until at last her spindle-thin legs were springing so fast that they could not be seen, and she seemed to be a ball of fur, twirling and whirling and blown by the wind.

Then Kangaroo Mouse reached tussocky grassland, and she stopped. She sat by a tuft of grass and said: 'It's twice as tall as myself *and* my tail, and it's thick and prickly. I can't go on. These kind of jumps are for *real* kangaroos.'

'Did you call me?' asked Kangaroo.

'No,' said Mouse. 'But I'm glad you're here. Go to the forest and take my message. A creature is coming down from the north. He has big shining scales and a beating tail, and he's walking along on his big strong legs.'

Kangaroo leapt towards the forest, crushing the grass beneath his feet. He came to the scrubland, and there he stopped. He saw spiky thickets, and thorny stems.

'Cassowary!' Kangaroo called. And out of the scrub came the great black bird. 'Cassowary, take my message. A creature is coming down from the north. He has great shining scales, and a huge beating tail, and he's marching along on his mighty legs.'

Cassowary turned to the scrub. He was not afraid of its spikes and thorns.

'I'm a fighting, biting, battling bird. I can push through worse than this,' he said.

He pushed and kicked through the spiky scrub, until he saw the forest ahead. He ran through the trees, and before very long he saw Bower Bird, Possum, Platypus, Turkey, and Wombat.

'Listen,' he said. 'Here is my message. A creature is

coming down from the north. He has huge shining scales, and a great lashing tail, and he's crashing along on enormous legs.'

The creatures stared at each other, and trembled.

'It's a dragon,' said Bower Bird.

'He'll eat us,' said Possum.

'Help!' said Platypus.

'Save us,' said Turkey.

'What a hullaballoo,' said Wombat.

Cassowary stamped his foot.

'You make me angry, you foolish creatures. Talking will do no good,' he said. 'Why don't you stir yourselves up, and *do* something?'

And he stamped away angrily back to the scrub.

'We must frighten the dragon away,' said Bower Bird.

'We must make a scarecrow to scare him,' said Possum.

'We don't want to scare a *crow*,' said Platypus.

'Then we'll make a scaredragon,' Turkey said.

'What a to-do and a fuss,' said Wombat.

They stuck the branch of a tree in the ground, for the scaredragon's body. Then they stuck a pineapple on to the branch, for the scaredragon's head.

But still they felt frightened.

'We must hide behind a wall,' said Bower Bird.

'And look out over the top,' said Possum.

'And when we hear the dragon coming, we'll shout, and wave our paws,' said Platypus.

'And make our faces look fierce,' said Turkey.

'What a hurry and scurry,' said Wombat.

The creatures began to make a wall.

They stuck a row of sticks in the ground, and Bower Bird, who knew about such things, fixed creepers and stems and twigs between them.

Possum banged the wall with his paw, to see if it was strong and safe.

Platypus filled the cracks with mud.

Turkey scraped up a pile of leaves, building them up behind the wall.

Wombat ran around in circles.

'Now we *ought* to be safe,' they said.

They stood in a row on the pile of leaves, looking out over the top of the wall.

And they waited, and waited, and waited.

Into the forest came little green Lizard, flicking his tiny tail in the air.

'Happy days!' he smiled to himself. 'I've come to the

28

forest. Oh, happy days!' And he pattered along on his stumpy legs.

'It's a long, long journey I've made,' he said. 'Over bushland and sand and grassland and scrub.'

He hopped in the air with a squeak of delight, because he felt happy and safe and friendly.

Then Lizard looked up.

And he saw the scaredragon.

'What is that pineapple doing?' he said. 'Just sitting quite still, all alone, on a stick?'

He saw the wall, and over the top of it, the faces of Bower Bird, Possum, Platypus, Turkey, and Wombat.

'And what are *you* doing, up there?' he asked.

The five faces stared back at little green Lizard.

'We're hiding away from the dragon,' said Bower Bird.

'He's coming down from the north,' said Possum.

'He'll eat us all up if he can,' said Platypus.

'He has huge shining scales, and a great lashing tail, and he's crashing along to the forest,' said Turkey.

'*What* a time we've had!' said Wombat.

Lizard's small scales shone green in the sun as he flicked his tiny tail in the air. Then he pattered behind the wall, and said:

'Please may I hide behind your wall? I'm not very fond of dragons, myself.'

So Bower Bird, Possum, Platypus, Turkey, Wombat, and Lizard looked out over the top of the wall, waiting for the dragon to come.

And they waited, and waited, and waited.

Far away, a dead branch fell, crashing to the forest floor.

'The dragon! It's coming,' the creatures cried.

They shouted, and flapped their paws about, and made fierce faces, until they were tired.

Then they all said: 'Sh!' and 'Listen!' and 'Hush!'

They kept very still behind the wall, and the only sound they heard was a plop! as a ripe red berry fell to the ground.

'Hurrah!' cried Bower Bird. 'We've done it! We've done it! We've scared the dreadful dragon away.'

'He's crashing back to the north,' said Possum.

'He'll never come *here* again,' said Platypus.

'We're really rather clever,' said Turkey.

'Clever and brave and fierce!' said Wombat.

Lizard did not say a word. He had disappeared behind a tree.

He looked at his little shining scales, and his flicking

tail and his stumpy legs.

He looked, and he thought very hard.

And he guessed.

'Oh my, I'm a dragon, I am!' he said. 'Oh ho! I'm a dragon. A great fierce dragon!'

Then Lizard flicked his tiny tail, and he rolled on the ground with his legs in the air, laughing and laughing and laughing.

Reginald's Lousy Adventure

Sarah Morcom

Reginald was a woodlouse. He was plump and black with fourteen little legs and a wavy pair of feelers, and he lived under a damp bit of skirting board in a kitchen wall. Reginald led a very sheltered sort of life. He was quite happy to spend most of his time quietly sitting under the skirting board with the other woodlice, enjoying the dark and damp. He didn't often go out, and when he did it was usually at night when he scuttled around looking for bits and pieces to eat. But he soon returned to his hidey-hole because he'd heard some rather nasty stories about what happened to woodlice who stayed outside too long.

But one day something happened that changed his quiet life completely – Reginald had an adventure! It all started when Mr Percy, the owner of the house, decided to have a brand new modern kitchen put in.

'We'll soon see the end of all this rising damp, dear,' said Mr Percy to Mrs Percy. 'They'll be ripping out that rotten skirting board tomorrow and putting in a nice, new damp-proof course. Then you'll be able to put some decent wallpaper up.'

The next day Mr Percy's kitchen was extremely noisy. Reginald and the other woodlice stayed very still in the dark wall, listening to the commotion and wondering what it was. They could sense something dangerous was going on and they felt uncomfortable.

Then, all of a sudden, there was a tearing, cracking noise and the skirting board was ripped away. The woodlice scattered in all directions as the light glared into their home. All, that is, except Reginald, who rolled himself into a petrified ball, afraid to move, with his little heart thumping as if it would burst. Something swept him out of the way roughly and he rolled across the floor, finally coming to rest against a cupboard. (It was a good thing he had his tough, outer coat to protect him or he would have been quite bruised.)

How long Reginald lay curled up there he didn't know. But it seemed a long time before all the banging and crashing around him stopped and he felt it was safe to move. Then he gingerly uncurled and took a peep around. The first thing he saw was a laundry basket full of washing. Reginald didn't know what it was, but all he wanted was somewhere to hide and it looked a reasonable sheltering-place. So he wriggled in among the clothes in the basket. To Reginald's surprise it was lovely and dark and damp and he crawled further into the folds of Mr Percy's checked shirt. Just like home, thought Reginald, and soon he felt so comfortable that he dropped off into a deep and peaceful sleep.

Poor Reginald didn't sleep for long! He was awoken by the most horrible, sick, dizzy feeling in his tummy and when he dared to open his eyes again he was not among the dark, wet clothes any more but seemed to be swinging in mid-air with the sun and earth dancing giddily before his eyes.

'Uuu-agh!' moaned Reginald. 'If this is flying, I don't like it.'

Meanwhile, Mrs Percy was singing as she hung the checked shirt with Reginald in it on the washing line. (She was in a good mood because of her new kitchen and too busy to notice the woodlouse clinging to the top of the pocket.)

'Zzzzz!' said a passing bee to Reginald. ''Ere, I wouldn't try stunts like that if I was you, mate. Could get yerself killed.'

Before he could catch his breath to reply, poor Reginald fell, exhausted, into the shirt pocket. For what seemed like hours he was flapped backwards and

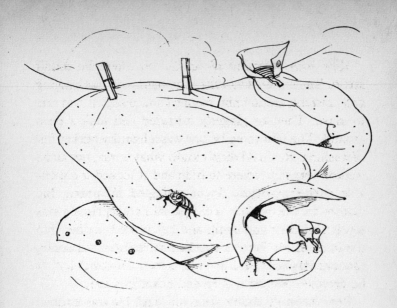

forwards and heaved up and down until he felt
thoroughly ill. What's more, the shirt was drying out
quickly in the breeze, and there is nothing that makes a
woodlouse feel worse than being dry. So, when at last
Mrs Percy unpegged the shirt from the line, Reginald
lay weak and gasping with thirst at the bottom of the
pocket, almost too ill to care what happened next.

But what happened next was more frightening by far.
Mrs Percy got her iron and ironing board out and, the
next moment, Reginald felt himself being thrown down
on to a hard, smooth surface that was even hotter and
drier than the washing line. Then . . . Boom! Something
heavy thundered down close to Reginald's ear and
blasted him with a cruel heat. In a flash Reginald knew
he must get out that very second or it would be too late.
He gathered all his remaining strength and scuttled out
of the shirt pocket, just as the gleaming, hot iron hissed
towards it.

'Ugh!' cried Mrs Percy, putting the iron down with a crash. 'Get away, you horrid thing!' And she swiped Reginald off the ironing board.

As he was falling, Reginald thought, This is the end. I can't take any more! He curled into a ball and shut his eyes . . .

There was a thud as Reginald hit the floor.

An anxious ladybird saw him fall and ran over. 'Oh, you poor thing, what a fall!' she twittered. 'Now don't move, dear. Just stay still and try to keep calm. Oh, dear, oh, dear, he's not speaking, he must be bad. Please say something, do!'

Reginald moaned and feebly flickered a feeler.

'Oh, thank goodness, he's still alive. Now, dearie – can you hear me? Where do you live and what's your name?'

'R-Reginald.'

'Reginald?' cried the ladybird. 'I know about you! They've been sending search parties out all day for you. Why, I was only talking to your family this morning. They were so worried that you'd been trodden on – come with me, dearie, and I'll show you where they are.'

Reginald waddled slowly along behind the ladybird. She led him out of the kitchen, into the garden to a large stone. Reginald peeped under it and there, huddled in the dark and looking very miserable, was his family.

And so Reginald's adventure ended. He and his family lived peacefully in the garden. And I'm pleased to say that their new home was much safer and quieter and they were never disturbed again.

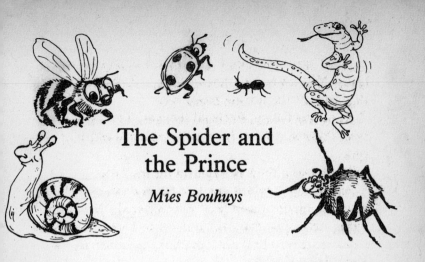

The Spider and
the Prince

Mies Bouhuys

One day, when the prince was still a baby in his cot, a
fairy visited the palace of his father the king. In her
hand she held a tiny golden box. As soon as she had
expressed her good wishes for the royal baby, she
disappeared as if by magic, leaving the golden box
behind. Full of curiosity the queen opened it, but she
immediately dropped it and turned pale. 'A spider!' she
cried. 'There's a spider in the box!'

All the members of the court retreated a step and the
ministers and ladies-in-waiting exchanged startled
glances. What did the good fairy mean by giving a
spider as a present? Could she not have thought of a
better gift for the baby prince than a fat brown spider
with a cross on its back?

One of the footmen brought a dustpan and brush to
sweep it up, but the king stopped him.

'No,' he said, 'the fairy must have had something
special in mind when she gave the prince this particular
present. Prepare a room for the spider.'

'A room?' Again the members of the court exchanged

glances, but of course the king's orders had to be obeyed. The most distant tower chamber was chosen for the spider, a room where nobody ever went. The eight walls of the room were covered in white satin and the spider could walk there to its heart's content.

And that is what happened. The spider was taken to the tower room by a particularly brave general. He locked the door and threw the key into the palace moat. Everyone heaved a sigh of relief, for now the spider could do no harm to anyone.

Nobody talked or even thought about it any more. But when the prince grew up, he did what every boy does sooner or later: he went exploring in his father's palace. He looked at all the portraits of his ancestors in the picture gallery and at the strange weapons in the armoury. He walked on tip-toe through the cellars filled with secret treasures and along the attics full of ancient, yellowing royal robes. And that is how one day he found the door of the tower chamber. He put his hand on the brass door-handle and tried to open it, but the door would not budge. Whoosh – the prince slid down the banisters to the room of the keeper of the Royal Keys and asked him for the key of the tower chamber.

'The tower chamber . . .?' the old Keeper said slowly. 'No, Your Highness, there is no key to that door.'

'Of course there is!' the little prince cried impatiently, for he was becoming curious. 'Every door has a key.'

But the Keeper of the Royal Keys was so old that he had long since forgotten the spider, and he continued to shake his head. Then the prince became furious. He tore the bunches of keys from the walls, threw them on the floor and almost hit the old keeper, who retired to a corner in alarm.

With his arms full of bunches of keys, the little prince ran up the stairs, and one by one he tried the keys in the lock of the tower chamber. When none of them fitted he became even angrier and he tore downstairs again, this time to the carpenter's workshop, where he picked up a hatchet. Back he ran upstairs and began to hack at the beautiful old oak door like a madman. He was absolutely determined to know what was behind that door. After an hour of hacking and battering, the door at last broke down and the little prince fell into the room.

He looked up, and immediately his anger vanished. In front of him he saw a white silk wall, on which a beautiful picture had been embroidered in tiny cross-stitches. Or rather, not one picture, but a hundred or more, all on that one wall. The little prince slowly rose to his feet. His eyes widened in amazement, for when he came nearer he saw himself in each of the pictures. First of all in his cot; next, playing with a toy bear. Every picture showed something that had really happened. Some of the pictures made him laugh and others made him feel happy because the prince in the picture looked happy. There were some that made the prince blush, because they showed him doing something that he shouldn't. But how had it happened? Who had embroidered all these pictures, these thousands upon thousands of tiny pictures?

His eyes strayed to the next wall. And then he had a shock. On the white silk wall a large spider with a shining white cross on its back was scurrying to and fro, embroidering tiny stitches faster than the eye could

follow. It was making another picture and the prince saw at a glance what it represented. It showed him, looking like a furious little monster, in the key-room, throwing keys about.

'No, no, don't!' cried the prince, for it suddenly occurred to him how terrible it would be if this ugly picture were to remain there for ever and ever. The spider interrupted its work for the fraction of a second and shook its head; and the prince understood what it meant. Anything that had ever happened to him would be pictured here for ever.

The prince did not say another word but silently stole down the stairs. After this he went up once a day to see what the cross-stitch spider had related about him on the white silk walls: bad things and good things, sad things and happy things. And every day, whenever he was about to do something naughty or stupid, the little prince stopped himself just in time when he thought of the spider up in the tower room.

And so he became the wisest and most sensible prince in the world, and on the day when he was to be crowned king, and walked up the steps of his palace with a beautiful young princess people noticed that he had had a little insect embroidered or painted on all his standards, arms and carriages.

'How strange!' people said. 'Why should the prince have chosen a cross-spider for an emblem?'

But the princess, who at that moment was standing with her prince on the threshold of the tower room, understood perfectly. For the cross-stitch spider had just started on another wall and was embroidering the next picture. It was the most beautiful picture of them all and it showed the prince and princess walking hand in hand in the sunshine in a landscape full of flowers and birds.

'That is how it should always be,' whispered the princess, and the prince nodded.

And that is how it happened. The new king and queen were the wisest and happiest rulers in the whole world. The cross-stitch spider had hardly enough silken thread to embroider so much happiness.

The Elephant
and the Beetle

Patricia Adams

There was once an elephant who was great friends with a beetle. One day the two friends made up their minds to go for a holiday by the sea.

They reached the seashore just as it was getting dark. The elephant picked up driftwood and made a fire. The beetle cooked their tea. Then they stayed up till very late, showing each other how they would swim in the sea.

Next morning the beetle woke up first. He nudged the elephant and together they rushed down to the sea. In went the beetle. He leaped and rolled and dived in the icy water.

But not the elephant.

As soon as he ran into the sea his feet began to sink into the soft, wet sand. Before he had time to think he was stuck fast in the sand. The waves lapped around his tummy.

He yelled to the beetle for help. The beetle tried everything he could think of, but he could not pull his friend out of the sand. While they pulled and tugged and pushed the tide rose slowly. It came higher and

43

higher. The two friends didn't know about tides. They thought the elephant was sinking down further into the sand.

Puffing, the beetle sat on the elephant's head to rest and to think. He saw a fish swim past the elephant's legs.

'Hey, Fish! Stop!' called the beetle. 'My friend is stuck in the sand, and I don't know how to get him out. Can you help?'

The fish looked up at the elephant's tail.

'When I want to move I flick my tail. It never fails.' And the fish swam off, with a flick of his scaly tail.

The beetle and the elephant looked at one another. They both nodded, and the elephant began to flick his little short tail. Nothing happened.

The tide rose a little higher.

'That fish didn't know what he was talking about,' snorted the beetle.

Just then a seagull dived into the water, and bobbed up near the two friends.

'Hey, Seagull! Stop!' yelled the beetle. 'My friend is stuck in the sand, and I don't know how to get him out. Can you help?'

The seagull looked up at the elephant's ears and said, 'When I want to move I flap my wings. It never fails.'

And, with a flap of his wings, he was gone.

The elephant and the beetle looked at one another.

'What a dope,' said the beetle. 'He doesn't mean wings. He must mean your ears.'

'Yes,' agreed the elephant. He began to flap his ears. He flapped and flapped. He flapped until he felt they would drop off. Nothing happened.

But the tide rose a little higher.

There was now more elephant under the water than there was above it.

The beetle was afraid. He sat on his friend's head and thought and thought. As he thought, the tide rose higher and higher. At last a tiny wave washed the beetle right off the elephant's head. At the same moment the elephant floated free of the sand.

'Hooray!' cried the elephant. 'I'm floating. I can swim. How very clever you are, Beetle. You knew it was your weight that was pushing me down into the sand!'

The beetle was very pleased at his friend's words. He was a clever beetle, indeed.

The Big Sore Toe

Joanne Horniman

Jenny thought it would be hard to find another boy as annoying as Johnny Watts. He lived down the road from her and so she would see him as they were walking to school, and on the way home as well.

Johnny liked shocking people – by eating orange peel, for example. Jenny always had an orange for lunch. It was peeled round and round, then wrapped up again in the curly peel. That way she just had to unwrap it at lunchtime.

Almost every day Johnny Watts would get the snake-like orange peel out of the garbage tin after Jenny had dropped it in. Then he'd eat it – not all of it. He'd just chew off a bit and eat that, then chew on the rest. Jenny could tell it was because he wanted to show off. He liked to hear the shrieks of disgust from the girls sitting near by. Once Jenny had offered it to him before she put it in the bin, but he refused. He liked to get it out of the bin to make people shudder.

He would bring creatures into the classroom and keep them in his desk to scare people with when the teacher was out of the room. Sometimes it would be a frog or a spider. One day he had brought a grub in a jar of dirt and said it was a witchetty grub. When he opened the bottle a horrible smell came out. The grub was dead.

On the way home from school he would walk near Jenny and say things to tease her. One afternoon he had stamped on a bee. Jenny had felt so sorry for the poor bee lying half dead on the grass that she picked it up. It stung her.

Yes, Johnny Watts was a mean, mean, mean, nasty boy.

But Jenny secretly admired the things he did. Sometimes she almost wished that she could do all the things that Johnny Watts did, to show him that she wasn't just weak.

Then something happened to change all that. Jenny got her chance. She was walking past Johnny's house. She looked up the side yard and could see Johnny at the back of the house swinging a funny wooden hammer with a very large square head.

It looked interesting. She felt bold, so she stepped into the garden and walked up the back yard.

'What are you doing?' she asked, trying to sound as if she didn't care.

Johnny didn't answer. He just looked up at her and went on swinging the hammer. He was knocking some stakes into the ground. She could tell he wasn't knocking the stakes in for any real purpose. He would hit them a few times; then pull them out.

'What is it?' she said.

'A mallet. Used to be my grandfather's.' He actually answered her this time.

At that moment a roar came from the house. 'What

are you doing with that mallet? Drop it at once! You're messing up the lawn.' It was Johnny's father.

Johnny dropped the mallet in shock. It fell on Jenny's big toe. She yelled in pain.

The mallet was heavy. But she didn't cry. She pulled her foot away, fighting the desire to burst into tears.

'You – you – *useless* boy!' she burst out crossly instead. Then she turned and went home.

Her toe swelled up. It got red. It went blue, then purple. Her toenail went black and then dropped off.

48

And she didn't cry once. She was secretly proud of her wound. It was so sore and swollen that she couldn't wear a shoe. Everyone knew that that stupid Johnny Watts had dropped a mallet on her toe, and that he wasn't supposed to be playing with it. They all saw how brave she was. She hadn't cried, or complained, even though her toe was so sore. Thanks to Johnny Watts she no longer had a big toenail.

Jenny began to think of herself in a new light. She was brave. She was courageous. She had scars to prove it.

Johnny didn't eat any orange peel for a few weeks after that. He didn't even bring any spiders into school. Not until Jenny's toe had healed anyway.

Then one day he appeared with a toad. An ugly, lumpy, little toad. 'He's holding it in his *hand!*' shrieked the girls.

But not Jenny. She fixed him with a look of scorn. She walked over and firmly reached out and took the toad. Johnny was so surprised he let her have it.

'What a silly thing to do. Leave the poor toad alone.' She placed the toad in a flower bed.

'Jenny took the toad from Johnny Watts!' exclaimed the girls with glee.

After that Jenny walked home from school in peace. Johnny didn't bother to tease her any more. She no longer secretly admired him for being able to pick up creepy-crawly creatures – it was easy and not at all scary when you did it.

But sometimes, when no one was looking, she would go into her garden, and pick up a frog or a grasshopper, just to keep in practice.

Dribble's House

Mies Bouhuys

Dribble the snail was crawling slowly along the muddy path towards the farm, carrying his pretty house on his back. His horns stood up as if he were searching the sky for something he urgently needed. And in fact that is exactly what he was doing. Dribble the snail was looking for the horse.

'Good morning, horse,' said Dribble, when at last he had found him. 'Won't you buy my house?'

'No,' said the horse, 'I have a perfectly good stable. What would I do with your house?'

Dribble the snail crawled on. He stopped when he saw the pig.

'Good morning, pig,' he said. 'Won't you buy my house?'

'No,' replied the pig, 'I already have a sty. What would I do with your house?'

Dribble the snail, the most stupid snail in the world, crawled on. He pricked up his horns and called to the pigeon in the pigeon loft. 'Good morning, pigeon. Won't you buy my house?'

'No,' the pigeon called back. 'I have a pigeon loft.

50

What would I do with your house?'

Dribble the snail crawled on. When he came to the henhouse he stopped again. 'Good morning, hen. Won't you buy my house?'

'No,' said the hen. 'I already have a chicken run and a henhouse and a nesting box. What would I do with your house?'

'But it's a very pretty house!' cried Dribble. 'Just the thing for you!'

Dribble was becoming somewhat impatient, so he was trying a little sales talk.

'Cluck-cluck,' said the hen. 'I can see it's a pretty house. But why do you want to sell it?'

'Because I should like a change,' said Dribble, the most stupid snail in the world. 'I'm looking for something a little bigger. If I could sell my house to one of you, I could buy a new one with the proceeds.'

'Well, yes,' said the hen, and she had another look at the snail's house. 'Oh well,' she said, 'it's a nice piece of grit. We don't get much grit nowadays. I'll buy your shell. It'll come in useful somehow. How much do you want for it?'

'What will you give me for it?' asked silly Dribble.

'Twenty grains of seed and twenty grains of corn,' said the cunning hen.

'It's a bargain,' said Dribble. He crept out of his shell, counted the twenty grains of seed and the twenty grains of corn which the hen gave him and crawled away as quickly as a snail with a bare back can crawl. Back to the horse.

'Good morning, horse. Do you happen to know of a house for sale?'

'How much can you pay?' asked the horse.

'Twenty grains of seed and twenty grains of corn.'

'That's not much to pay for a house, Dribble, but I'll give it some thought.'

Lowering his head, the horse began to think.

Dribble crawled on to the pig and asked him the same question. The pig didn't think it was a very good price to offer either, but he promised to think about it. He lay down with his snout in the mud and began to think.

Dribble meanwhile had reached the pigeon loft. The pigeon, too, began to think, her head tucked under her wing.

Dribble crawled on, looking for a house, but wherever he looked he couldn't find one or even someone who knew of one for sale.

The sun went down, the wind rose, it started to rain,

and Dribble felt the cold on his back. How he missed his lovely warm shell, in which he could curl up completely!

Once more he visited the animals, one by one. 'Have you thought about it, horse? Have you thought, pig? Have you thought, pigeon?'

They all shook their heads. Dribble, the most stupid snail in the world, crawled on, trembling with cold. Suddenly he stopped. He had found another animal. It was hanging in a shiny web of silver threads between the sunflowers in the farmhouse garden.

'Hello, spider,' said Dribble. 'Do you by any chance know of a house for sale?'

'Indeed I do,' said the spider, who had dropped to the bottom thread of the cobweb and was swaying to and fro just above Dribble's head. 'Indeed I know of a house for

sale. I'm just about to move myself, you see. As soon as I've found somewhere else to live you can have my house.'

'Splendid! Splendid!' Dribble would have danced for joy if he had been able to. 'What do you want for your house, spider?'

'What can you give me for it?'

'Twenty grains of seed and twenty grains of corn, spider.'

The spider made a wry face. 'What would I do with twenty grains of seed and twenty grains of corn?' he asked.

'Oh, please, please . . .' pleaded Dribble. 'I do want a house so badly. I've already sold my old one, you see.'

'Oh well, all right,' said the spider. 'For twenty grains of seed and twenty grains of corn the hen will sell me a corner of the henhouse. It's warm, with lots of flies and midges, and there's plenty of room for my web.'

'Fine, fine,' cried Dribble. 'Tell me quickly where your house is.'

'You're definitely buying it?' asked the spider, dropping to the ground.

'Naturally,' said Dribble. 'It's a bargain!'

'Well, come in then,' said the spider, and he pointed to the cobweb with one of his numerous legs.

'What!' cried Dribble. 'Do you call that a house?'

But the spider had already gone and was well on the way to the warm hen-house. All that silly Dribble could do was to climb up the silver threads and perch in the middle of the cobweb. The wind was even colder up there, and the rain trickled down his bare back. It was then that Dribble began to realize that he was the most stupid snail in the world. And as soon as he saw that, he dropped down from the cobweb and crawled, as fast as he could, back to the hen.

'Hen, hen, can I buy my house back?'

The hen was just taking her first peck at the snail shell. Over her head the spider was busily spinning a web in the corner of the henhouse, for which he had paid twenty grains of seed and twenty grains of corn. If the hen hadn't happened to be in a good mood because she had got her seed and her corn back, she might have said no. But now she agreed. 'All right, then,' she said. And with her yellow toe she pushed the snail shell over to Dribble. Overjoyed, he crawled in, and with his house on his back he went to see the horse, the pig and the pigeon.

'Hello, horse. Hello, pig. Hello, pigeon. You can stop thinking. I don't want to move to another house after all. I don't want any house except my own.'

'Good,' said the horse, the pig and the pigeon. 'Goodbye, Dribble!'

'Goodbye, all!' said Dribble, but nobody heard him, for he had disappeared into the pretty house on his back.

Mr Learn-a-lot and The Singing Midges

Alf Prøysen

One warm summer night Mrs Midge said to her daughters, 'We'll go and visit Mr Learn-a-lot, the schoolmaster.'

'What do we want to do that for?' asked the young midges. There were three of them: Big Sister Midge, Middle Sister Midge, and Wee Sister Midge.

'We're going to sing to him. You're all so good at singing now, it's a pleasure to listen to you, and Mr Learn-a-lot is such a good judge of music.'

So they all flew off to Mr Learn-a-lot's house and hovered outside his bedroom window. Mrs Midge peered through the glass while her daughters all talked at once in high, squeaky voices:

'Is the window shut, Mama?'

'Won't he open it, Mama?'

'Can't we get in, Mama?'

'I expect he'll open the window when he goes to bed,' said Mrs Midge.

'He's opening the window now, Mama!'

'Can we go in now, Mama?'

'What shall we sing for him, Mama?'

'Not so fast, children, there's no hurry. Let Mr Learn-a-lot get nicely into bed first.'

'He's climbing into bed now, Mama! He's in bed, really he is, Mama! Wouldn't it be dreadful if he fell asleep before he heard our singing, Mama?' squeaked all the little midges. But Mrs Midge was sure the schoolmaster would wake up again when they started singing.

'I think Big Sister Midge had better go in first,' she said.

'All right, but what am I to sing, Mama?'

'You can sing the song about "We midges have not got ...",' said Mrs Midge, and settled herself with her two younger daughters behind the curtain. 'And remember to fly in a circle over his head. If he likes your song he will sit up in bed. Now off you go!'

And Big Sister Midge flew round and round in a circle over Mr Learn-a-lot's head and sang this song:

'We midges have not got a couple of beans
Yet in summer we all are as happy as queens,
For every night in a swoon of delight
We dance to the tune of our dizzy flight,
And all we need to keep in the pink
Is a tiny drop of your blood to drink.'

Three times she sang the same verse, and she was beginning to think Mr Learn-a-lot didn't care for her song at all. But suddenly he sat bolt upright in bed.

'Come back! Come back, child!' whispered Mrs Midge.

'Was I all right, Mama?'

'You were very good. Now we'll just wait till Mr

Learn-a-lot has fallen asleep again, then it'll be Middle Sister's turn. You can sing the song about "How doth the little busy me" – that is so very funny! There! Now I think it would be all right for you to start. But you mustn't leave off before Mr Learn-a-lot has got right out of bed and is standing in the middle of the floor. Fly a little higher than your sister did. Off you go!'

And Middle Sister Midge sang as loudly as she could while she flew round and round the schoolmaster's head:

> 'How doth the little busy me
> Improve each shady hour
> By settling on your nose or knee
> As if upon a flower.'

She hadn't sung more than one verse before Mr Learn-a-lot threw off the bedclothes and tumbled out of bed.

'Come back, come back!' whispered Mrs Midge.

'Wasn't I good?' said Middle Sister as she arrived back all out of breath. 'And I wasn't a bit afraid of him!'

'That'll do; we midges are not in the habit of boasting,' said Mrs Midge. 'Now it's Wee Sister's turn.'

'What shall I sing?' asked the smallest midge with the tiniest voice you ever heard.

'You can sing our evening song – you know – the one that goes:

> 'The day is done and all rejoice
> To hear again this still small voice.
> May the music of my wings
> Console you for my little stings.

'That's just the thing for tonight,' Mrs Midge added thoughtfully.

'Oh yes, I know that one,' said Wee Sister; she was very pleased her mother had chosen one she knew.

'I expect it will be the last song tonight,' said Mrs Midge, 'and don't worry if you don't get right through it. If Mr Learn-a-lot suddenly claps his hands you must be sure to come back to me at once. Will you remember that?'

'Yes, Mama,' said Wee Sister, and off she flew.

Mr Learn-a-lot was lying absolutely still. So Wee Sister began to sing – all on one top note:

'*The day is done*'

Smack! Mr Learn-a-lot clapped his hands together.

'Come back, come back!' called Mrs Midge. But there was no sign of Wee Sister.

'Oh, my darling, sweet wee one, please come back to your mother!' wailed Mrs Midge. No sound – no sound at all for a long time; then suddenly Wee Sister was sitting on the curtain beside them.

'Didn't you hear me calling?' asked Mrs Midge very sternly.

'Oh yes, but you said I was to fly very, very quietly, and that clap of Mr Learn-a-lot's sent me flying right into the darkest corner of the room.'

'Poor darling!' said Mrs Midge. 'But you're safe back now. You've all been very good and very clever girls. And now I'd like to hear what you think of Mr Learn-a-lot?'

Big Sister answered, 'He's nice; he likes the one who sings longest best!'

Middle Sister answered, 'He's very polite; he gets out of bed for the one who sings loudest!'

And Wee Sister said, 'I think he's very musical; he claps the one with the sweetest voice!'

'Yes, yes, that's all very true,' said Mrs Midge; 'but now I will tell you something else about Mr Learn-a-lot. He is not only a very learned gentleman, but he will provide us with the nicest, most enjoyable supper, and we needn't even wake him up. Shall we go?'

'Oh, that is a fine idea!' cried Big Sister, Middle Sister, and Wee Sister Midge, for they always did just what their mother told them.

Poor Mr Learn-a-lot!

Spider's Surprise

Sarah Morcom

Old Mag the hag was a witch. She was very old and ugly with a runny eye and a moustache, and you could smell her coming a mile off. Old Mag lived in a dreadful cottage called The Dumps. (The name suited it very well.)

Also in The Dumps lived Black Bert. Black Bert was the fattest, hairiest, dirtiest spider in the neighbourhood and he lived in a dark corner of Old Mag's kitchen. He thought he was very important and bullied all the other spiders so they were afraid of him. All day long he sat lazily on his filthy web, giving orders and surveying his domain like a fat king. Sometimes he would sidle off on his hairy legs to take up position by the front door, where he acted as chief bouncer, frightening off any creepy-crawly that dared to go near (and usually eating it afterwards). Old Mag had a soft spot for Black Bert. She let him ride around on her hat occasionally, which he thought was a great treat, and he particularly enjoyed crawling behind her ear.

One day, Old Mag bought a magazine. It was called *WITCH – The Mag for the Modern Hag*. She sat down and put on her smeary spectacles to read it.

' 'Ere, wot's she readin'?' croaked Black Bert, who was a nosey old spider. 'Go 'n' 'ave a look, will yer.' He ordered one of the young spiders to go and spy on Old Mag to see what she was reading.

The young spider let himself nimbly down on his thread over Old Mag's head. But what he saw on the page nearly made him fall on to Old Mag's lap in fright. It read:

SPIDER SOUFFLÉ – A NEW REMEDY FOR THE AGEING WITCH
Capture your lost youth with this delicious tonic – tasty and effective – knocks years off your life!

INGREDIENTS
One fully-matured spider (as large and juicy as possible)
Two tablespoonfuls medium-sized spiders
½ teaspoon money spiders
¾ pint slug slime . . .

The young spider read no further – he had seen enough to make him feel most uncomfortable. He quickly returned to Black Bert, quite sure they were going to be eaten.

'Nah, she ain't gonna cook us, stupid,' growled Black Bert. 'She'll use them imported ones from outside.'

Black Bert sounded very sure, but underneath he was really quite frightened, because they all knew that imported spiders were thought to be tough and tasteless.

The next day, further alarming things began to happen. Old Mag seemed to be in a very strange mood. She pottered round the cottage tidying things up, and even dusted away some of the larger cobwebs. Black Bert was furious at this disturbance to his filthy home. At tea time Old Mag did something unbelievable for her – she washed her hair! I won't tell you what sort of things came out of it into the water (it might put you off your next meal), but the sink was blocked for days afterwards. Then the spiders watched, amazed, as she laid the table for two with her best black china and a vase of deadly nightshade and stinkweed as a centre-piece. That evening a young, rather greasy-looking wizard called at The Dumps, and he and Old Mag sat down to a candle-lit dinner. They leered at each other and held hands across the table, and Black Bert didn't like it one bit.

Over the next few days the young wizard visited very often. Old Mag seemed to have forgotten about Black

Bert altogether. She no longer asked him to ride on her hat and instead spent all her time dressing up and making herself look fancy for her wizard boyfriend. All this put Black Bert in a nasty temper and he took it out on the younger spiders, making their lives a daily misery.

Then, one morning, one of Black Bert's spies came rushing to him in a state of extreme panic. 'She's got the spider recipe out again and the pot's already on the boil. We're done for now!'

Black Bert thought quickly. 'All right you lot, keep yer 'eads on. This calls for Emergency Operations. Go 'n' get the Black Box an' don't mess about!'

Only Black Bert knew what was in the Black Box. On it was printed TOP SECRET in large letters. Black Bert took a rusty old key and opened it up. Inside was a large package marked CAUTION: OPEN IN EMERG-ENCY ONLY. With the package was a dirty sheet of paper covered with spidery writing. It read:

SPIDER SUPERGLUE: THE ULTIMATE DEFENSIVE WEAPON FOR SPIDERS
Instructions for making superglue:

1   Eat as much of enclosed confectionery as possible
2   Spin webs in normal way.

Black Bert ripped open the parcel and there, in a sticky, glistening pile, was an enormous quantity of wine gums.

'Right, mates,' said Black Bert. 'Get stuck into this lot and FAST!'

Immediately the pile of wine gums was covered with a

wriggling mass of spiders, all tearing and chomping at the sweets. Black Bert sat in the middle, dribbling and smacking his lips in an unsavoury manner. When they'd finished, the spiders felt very full, and extremely sticky.

'Now then, comrades,' said Black Bert with a loud belch. 'Back to your stations and get spinnin'!'

Meanwhile Old Mag was getting the pot nice and hot for the Spider Soufflé. She read the recipe out loud to herself: 'One fully-matured spider – Ah yes . . .'

She went over to the dark corner where Black Bert lived, with a nasty smile on her face. 'Bertie! Bertie, darling. How would you fancy a little ride on Auntie Mag's hat today? Come out, dearie, and say hello to your Auntie.'

Black Bert bounced back into the shadows, grinning a horrible grin. Old Mag poked at him with her finger and immediately a mass of sticky web stuck to it. (Black Bert's web was made of Spider superglue!)

Old Mag pulled the curtain aside and got quite a shock – the curtain stuck to her hand! She pulled hard but it wouldn't budge.

Old Mag stamped her foot and muttered some nasty words under her breath. Finally she gave a great yank and brought the curtain pole clanging down. She fell back on to a chair, cursing and grumbling, and in his corner, Black Bert sat smiling and rubbing his hairy front legs together in a quiet satisfaction.

Meanwhile, the other spiders had been weaving their superglue webs with great speed all over the kitchen, covering every piece of furniture they could find. So when Old Mag tried to get up, she found the chair stuck firmly to her bottom. At that moment, the doorbell rang

and Black Bert slunk away to answer it. It was Old
Mag's boyfriend and he was just in time to see Old Mag
give a last, furious tug at the chair, ripping her skirt off
with it. There she stood in her baggy, black bloomers,
showing her horrible, warty legs. I'm afraid to say she
looked so ridiculous that the wizard couldn't stop
himself laughing.

Old Mag was so angry it looked as if she would burst
– her face was purple. 'Get out!' she screamed at the
wizard. 'Get out! And you needn't come back again!'

Then she turned to Black Bert. 'I think this is all your
doing, you creepy little insect. Get rid of this stuff
immediately or I'll turn you into – into—'

'Spider Soufflé?' said Black Bert with a leery smile.
'That's wot you was goin' to turn us all into, wasn't it,
dear Auntie Mag? And until you promise to leave us

alone an' treat us respec'ful-like, I'm afraid you'll 'ave a sticky time of it.'

'All right, I promise, I promise,' said Old Mag, dragging the rug with her. (She'd stuck to that now.)

By the time all the spiders had mixed the special paste to unstick the superglue, Old Mag looked like a walking scrapyard, with half her kitchen stuck to her. She didn't get rid of the wizard as quickly as she would have liked either, for in trying to get out, he'd stuck to the doorhandle.

So that is how Black Bert showed Old Mag he was not going to be made into Spider Soufflé and ruled the kitchen once more. Mag went back to her old, dirty ways again, but she was always very polite to any spider she saw, for fear of meeting a sticky end!

Big Spider gets a Fright

Elizabeth Robinson

Big Spider was enormous! He had a fat, hairy body, eight eyes that swivelled so that he could look backwards as well as forwards, and eight very long legs. When they saw Big Spider lurking in a dark corner, or running across the carpet, people often shuddered in horror. Others even squealed in terror and ran away. Big Spider liked it best of all when they did this – he was never happier than when he was frightening someone.

Who shall I frighten today, he wondered, as he admired himself in the window of the conservatory which was his home.

Jane was singing as she washed the breakfast dishes in the kitchen. She did not know about Big Spider yet, she had only arrived yesterday.

Big Spider hurried on his eight very long legs to the kitchen, and he climbed on to the windowsill above the sink. He grinned his leeriest, scariest grin, and waited for Jane to see him, and to run away squealing in terror.

Jane went on singing, and she dried the dishes without glancing once in the direction of the windowsill.

'Come on! Look at me,' said Big Spider impatiently.

Jane put the last dry cup on its hook on the shelf of the dresser, and went into the sitting room, to dust.

'Drat!' exclaimed Big Spider crossly.

Big Spider ran on his eight very long legs to the sitting room, and settled himself on top of the bookcase. He grinned his leeriest, scariest grin, and waited for Jane to come and dust the bookcase, and to see him, and to run away squealing in terror.

Jane dusted the small tables, and the arms of the chairs. Then she came towards the bookcase. Almost there, she stopped to give the door knob a good hard rub with her duster.

'Come on! Come and dust the bookcase,' said Big Spider impatiently.

Jane began to walk towards the bookcase once more, but the telephone rang in the hall, and she hurried to answer it. When she had finished talking on the telephone, Jane forgot about dusting the bookcase, and went upstairs to make the beds.

'Drat!' exclaimed Big Spider crossly.

Big Spider ran on his eight very long legs upstairs, and settled himself on the head of Jane's bed in the small bedroom. He grinned his leeriest, scariest grin, and waited for Jane to come and see him, and to run away squealing in terror.

First, Jane made the bed in the big front bedroom.

'Come on!' said Big Spider impatiently. 'Come and make your bed.'

Next, Jane made the bed in the big back bedroom.

'Come on!' said Big Spider impatiently. 'Come and make your bed.'

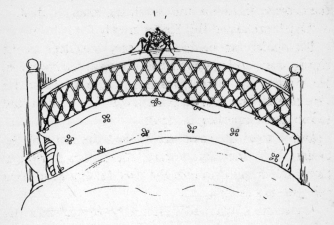

At last Jane came to make her bed in the small bedroom. She put out her hand to plump up the pillow . . .

Now she will see me, thought Big Spider gleefully.

At that moment the doorbell rang, and Jane hurried to open the door. Jane's friend Sara had come to visit her. Jane forgot about making her bed, and she invited Sara in for a cup of coffee.

'Drat!' exclaimed Big Spider crossly. Then he thought how much more fun it would be to frighten two people, instead of one. He ran on his eight very long legs down the stairs, and into the sitting room, where he settled himself in the middle of the coffee table. He grinned his leeriest, scariest grin, and waited for Jane and Sara to see him, and to run away squealing in terror. Big Spider could hardly wait!

At last Jane and Sara came into the sitting room. Jane was carrying a tray with the coffee on it, and Sara was carrying a plate with biscuits on it. Jane bent to put the tray on the coffee table. Sara bent to put the plate on the coffee table. They both saw Big Spider . . . .

'Oh!' exclaimed Jane. 'What a beautiful spider!'

'Oh, yes!' exclaimed Sara. 'Let's find a box to put him in, and keep him for a pet!'

Big Spider squealed in terror, and ran away as fast as his eight very long legs would take him, back to the conservatory where he lived.

Tumf

W.J. Corbett

For six days of the week Tumf was an ordinary young elephant. On those days he lived inside a circle of aunts and was pampered and spoiled, for they loved him dearly.

'Only the ripest bananas for Tumf,' they would say. 'And the plumpest, for he wishes to grow big and strong like his father.'

Sometimes his mother would squeeze into the circle for a glimpse of her son. Anxiously she would say, 'I hope Tumf isn't being ruined with all this attention.'

Gently she would be squeezed out again. 'We know what is best for Tumf,' the aunts would reply. 'Another hand of bananas for our precious.'

Tumf endured all the fuss. When he was quite full he would settle down to play with his drum. The hollow log provided by the aunts made a delightful sound when tapped smartly with the tip of his trunk, 'Tumf' it would go. And, more tunefully, 'Tumf ti tumf tumf,' for he was skilled at making up tunes. And his aunts would sway with enjoyment for they loved both him and his music. And so for those six days of the week he lived his life deep in the jungle, deep inside the circle of adoring aunts. All except for Tuesdays.

Tuesdays were special. They were Tumf's days for pretending and dreaming. Each Tuesday morning he would wander off alone and become something else until the sun went down. Last Tuesday he had imagined himself a beautiful white bird with a yellow beak. All that day he had soared and hovered over the tree-tops, feeling as light and as free as thistledown. But his day had been a little spoiled. For if there was one thing Tumf hated it was for someone to play his drum without his permission.

'Tumf tumf tumf' the sound of his drum came floating out of the jungle. It was his aunts calling him home, for the sun was going down. Reluctantly he had obeyed the call.

'And what were we today?' they asked, plying him with bananas. 'A beautiful white bird with a yellow beak? Well, we never. And did you miss us dreadfully?'

'Tumf tumf tumf' the annoyed young elephant shook his head as he tapped out tunes on his drum.

Soon Tuesday came around again. 'Today I shall be a little black ant,' he said to himself. So saying, he set off for the Plain where the ants built castles in the sun. Whilst marching along behind the soldier ants he had a visitor.

'And what have we here?' asked the green spider with glittering eyes. Just passing, his curiosity had been aroused by Tumf's strange behaviour.

'I'm a little black ant,' explained the young elephant. 'It's Tuesday, you see.'

'I never doubted it,' replied the green spider, squat-

74

ting comfortably upon his many hairy legs. 'It so happens Tuesday is my special day too. Especially Tuesday teatime. For guess what I fancy for tea on Tuesdays?'

Tumf said he was much too busy to play guessing games. A little black ant's work was never done, he declared.

The green spider watched with amusement as Tumf crawled about amongst the castles. For their part the real ants thought him a thorough nuisance, but kept their distance for fear of being rolled on.

'Well, I'll tell you,' said the spider, with a grin. 'There is nothing quite so tasty as little black ants for Tuesday teatime. What do you think about that? Are you terribly afraid?'

Tumf certainly was. Now he was wishing he was a young elephant again, safe in the jungle, safe in the circle of his aunts. He fearfully watched as the green spider, still broadly smiling, rose to his toes and advanced. With a loud trumpet Tumf scrambled up and began to lumber away as fast as he could go.

'Lovely grub,' yelled the spider, entering into the spirit of things. He hadn't had so much fun in ages. He set off in pursuit.

Tumf, still living out his fantasy, was now a badly frightened little black ant. His blind dash across the Plain soon led him to the brink of disaster. Only just in time did he manage to check his flight, as suddenly before him yawned the Bottomless Gorge, waiting to swallow another victim. For one awful moment Tumf teetered on the edge. Wildly glancing behind he saw the green spider, eyes glittering, jaws ravening for tea.

Then suddenly a slender ray of hope was offered to a little black ant. For across the gorge from lip to lip trembled a single strand of spider web, shimmering in the setting sun. Delicate and fine, it could not possibly be swarmed by a fat green spider with glittering eyes. But a little black ant . . . Tumf leaned forward, his foot reaching out to tread that path to salvation. No longer was the spider grinning. On his face was now a look of horror, for what had begun as a joke seemed about to end in a death. Then suddenly it was dusk, and . . . .

'Tumf, tumf, tumf' across the Plain came the sound of his drum calling him home. Abruptly Tumf drew back from the void. Turning, he lumbered off, feeling extremely annoyed. He did so wish his aunts wouldn't play his drum without permission. He also felt angry about the fat green spider with glittering eyes. Tumf hated to have his daydreams interrupted by strangers. He decided that next Tuesday he would pretend to be an extra-large black spider with evil eyes who enjoyed green spiders for tea. That would teach a certain someone a lesson. Some time later an exceedingly lucky young elephant arrived safely home.

The moon rode high, as deep in the jungle a circle was filled, and the tropical air vibrated with the sound of a solemnly rhythmic, 'tumf tumf tumf . . . tumf ti tumf tumf' on a drum . . . .

Little Fly
on the Ceiling

Angela Pickering

Are you sitting comfortably? Then I'll begin.

The little fly was walking on the ceiling. From the corner by the door to the corner by the window. From the corner by the window to the corner by the door.

'Little fly, little fly,' yawned the cat on the rug, 'why do you walk on the ceiling?'

The little fly walked across the ceiling to the lampshade. He hung upside down by his sticky feet and looked at the cat on the rug.

'Zzzzzz. Why shouldn't I walk on the ceiling if I want to?'

'No reason,' said the cat on the rug, 'no reason at all. I just wondered why, that's all. *Most* of us walk on the ground.'

'Ah,' said the little fly. 'Then most of you can't see the table, Grandpa's table laid ready for tea.'

He walked across the ceiling to the corner by the cupboard. From the corner by the cupboard to the corner by the shelf.

'Little fly, little fly,' yawned the cat on the rug, 'that's not a reason. Grandpa would never invite you for tea.

Why, tell me why, do you walk on the ceiling?'

'Zzzzzz. Why shouldn't I walk on the ceiling if I want to?'

'No reason,' said the cat on the rug, 'no reason at all. I just wondered why, that's all. *Most* of us walk on the ground.'

'Ah,' said the little fly, 'then most of you can't see Grandpa's pot plants growing on the sill.'

He walked across the ceiling. From the corner by the shelf to the corner by the cupboard. From the corner by the cupboard to the corner by the shelf.

'Little fly, little fly,' yawned the cat on the rug, 'that's not a reason. Grandpa's plants will grow no matter how high you are. Why, tell me why, do you walk on the ceiling?'

'Zzzzzz. Why shouldn't I walk on the ceiling if I want to?'

'No reason,' said the cat on the rug, 'no reason at all. I just wondered why, that's all. *Most* of us walk on the ground.'

'Ah,' said the little fly, 'then most of you can't see the top of Grandpa's shiny head. Such a smooth bald head it is. No hair left at all. I would like to settle on Grandpa's shiny head.'

'Little fly, little fly,' yawned the cat on the rug, 'that's not a reason. Grandpa would never let you settle on his shiny bald head. Why, tell me why, do you walk on the ceiling?'

'Ah,' said the little fly, 'so many questions. Do you really want to know why I walk on the ceiling?'

'Well,' yawned the cat, 'it's what I keep asking.'

The little fly walked across the ceiling. From the

corner by the shelf to the corner by the door. From the corner by the door to the very very middle. Right over the mat where the cat was sitting.

'Zzzzzz,' said the little fly. 'I walk on the ceiling so that Grandpa's cat cannot swot me with its paw. Zzzzzz. That's why!'

And then the little fly sang this song:

The Little Fly's Song

I get a kind of feeling
When I'm walking on the ceiling
That the cat is waiting for me down below.
My head is kind of reeling
When I'm walking on the ceiling,
I am better up, and down I will not go.
I would rather not be squealing
On the mat. For on the ceiling
Is the safest place of all I surely know.
I've a squealing kind of feeling,
And a reeling kind of feeling,
And a wheeling kind of feeling,
When I'm walking on the ceiling,
For the cat is waiting for me down below.

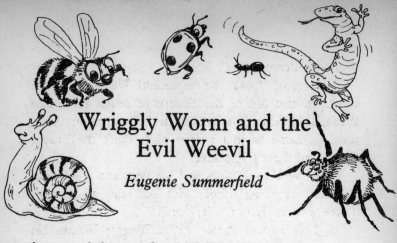

Wriggly Worm and the Evil Weevil

Eugenie Summerfield

Are you sitting comfortably? Then I'll begin.

'Wriggly Worm! Wriggly Worm!'

It was the little Brown Snails calling. They sounded rather upset.

'What's the matter?' asked Wriggly Worm, as the little Brown Snails crowded round him.

'It . . . it's that *thing*, over there,' cried the smallest of the Brown Snails.

'It's that Evil Weevil. He's in our playground and he's causing trouble. We're afraid to play there any more.'

Then all the Brown Snails cried very loudly.

'Oh, he is, is he? I'll soon settle him,' said Wriggly Worm.

The little Brown Snails stopped crying at once and pressed around Wriggly Worm even closer.

'What will you do, Wriggly? Are you going to fight him?'

'If I have to!' answered Wriggly Worm bravely, even though this Evil Weevil was probably very big and very fearsome. 'In your playground did you say? Then I think I'll just go across and find out what that horrible

Weevil is doing.'

To cries of 'Oooh, do be careful Wriggly!' off he went. In and out of the clumps of rough grass and through the fallen leaves under the horse chestnut trees, until he came to that special part where the Brown Snails had their playground.

There were twig slides and see-saws and a splendid tree-bark climbing frame, with leaf mats all around. There was no sign of Evil Weevil.

'Is there anyone there?' called Wriggly Worm. No answer.

Then, from underneath the leaf mats in front of the climbing frame came a crunching, chewing noise.

'Is that you, Evil Weevil?' called Wriggly Worm.

This time there was a nasty horrible laugh, but still no sign of Evil Weevil.

Wriggly Worm became rather cross.

'If you really are an Evil Weevil, why don't you come out and show yourself?' he called.

The leaf mats moved – just a little. Then, from underneath the leaves came crawling a creature so small it could hardly be seen at all.

'So you're Evil!' said Wriggly Worm.

He was astonished to find this creature was neither big nor fearsome after all.

'Yes, I am,' said Evil Weevil, trying to sound important. '*And* I'm a cousin of the great Boring Woodbeetle, I am,' he said, although he had never actually met Boring.

'Well, what are you doing in the Brown Snails' playground?' demanded Wriggly Worm.

'Eating,' snapped Evil Weevil and began chewing the

side of the climbing frame again. 'I don't know anything about playgrounds. But these are some of the most tasty pieces I've found for miles around.'

And he laughed his nasty, horrible laugh again.

'Stop it! Stop it at once,' yelled Wriggly Worm. 'If you keep on like that, there'll be nothing left of the little Brown Snails' playground.'

'But I'm hungry!' complained Evil Weevil. 'And I can't help it. I always laugh like that when I'm hungry. Perhaps you can tell me where else I can get a good feed.'

'Yes,' said Wriggly Worm, 'as a matter of fact, I can. Your cousin Boring's home is full of all kinds of rare delights. That's where you should go. Why don't you pay him a visit?'

Evil Weevil didn't seem to be too certain about this.

'Yes, well . . .' he giggled nervously, 'I am only a very distant cousin. Boring is so much higher up in the family tree. He may not welcome a visit from a humble weevil like me.'

'Oh, nonsense,' declared Wriggly Worm, 'I know Boring very well indeed and I'll arrange for you to meet him.'

Evil Weevil was greatly impressed. He forgot to chew. He forgot to laugh his horrible laugh.

'Would you? Could you?' was all he could say.

'Yes, well,' said Wriggly Worm. 'First of all you must mend the little Brown Snails' climbing frame.'

'Oh sure!' replied Evil Weevil eagerly and set to work. So in no time at all Wriggly Worm and Evil Weevil were crawling across to Boring's imposing residence. Then Wriggly Worm shouted, 'Boring,

there's someone here who's dying to meet you.'

'Oh, jolly good show,' Boring called back, as he came flying down at once from his lofty attic. And 'Tophole chaps!' when Wriggly Worm had introduced him to Evil Weevil.

Boring was delighted to meet a distant cousin. He would be able to tell him all the thousand Boring family stories he knew if Evil Weevil would come to stay with him.

'Look, I say, Evily Weevily old thing, you must come and stay with me for just as long as you like,' said Boring.

And Evil Weevil, who had never heard any of Boring's stories before, was delighted. So he stayed with Boring all through the long and dreary winter.

As for Wriggly Worm, he told the little Brown Snails, 'There's no Evil Weevil now in your playground. You can play there again whenever you like.'

They all said, 'Oh, thank you, Wriggly Worm, you are wonderful.'

And of course, he is, isn't he?

The Box

Marion Spring

Once there was a box.

Jim was walking down the road when he found the box. What was inside it?

Jim picked up the box. It wasn't heavy, so he carried it all the way home.

Jim put his box on the kitchen table.

Then Jim took a good look at the box. Jim smelt the box . . . Jim listened to the box. And he knew what was hiding inside.

Jim's mother arrived home with her shopping. 'What do you have inside that box, Jim?' she asked.

Jim answered her quietly, 'A dragon.'

Jim's mother tried not to look too surprised. 'A dragon? How do you know? Have you looked inside your box?'

'No,' said Jim, 'but I can hear him scratching. He's inside, trying to scratch his way out. So look out!'

Jim's mother put her ear close to the box and she listened. 'I can hear something scratching,' she whispered. Then all was quiet. 'I can't hear him any more, Jim. Is he all right?'

'He's going to have a sleep now. He's tired of scratching,' Jim answered.

Jim sang a quiet, sleepy song to the dragon in the box.

'Sleep, sleep, dragon dear.

Sleep, sleep, I am here.

Sleep, sleep, sleep.'

Jim's father came home from work 'Evening, Son. What do you have inside that box?

'Hi, Dad.' Jim took some time before he said, 'It's a furry monster.'

Jim's father blinked. 'Did you say a furry monster? How do you know, Son? Have you looked in the box?'

'No,' said Jim, but I can hear him breathing loud, slow, monster breaths. Listen . . . .'

Jim's father moved close to the box and listened. 'I can hear something breathing, Jim, but it doesn't seem to be making any other sound. Why not?'

'He's frightened of your loud voice and he's hiding,' answered Jim. 'He'll be all right if I talk to him for a while.'

So, very softly, Jim whispered to the frightened monster in the box. 'Don't be frightened of my dad. He won't hurt you, Furry Monster. He's just a bit too noisy at times. You're safe in your box.'

Jim's big sister was late getting home from school. 'What have you got inside the box, Jimbo?'

Jim waited till he knew she was listening, then he told her, 'A robot.'

'Oh yeah! And how do you know it's a robot? Have

you looked inside the box?' She didn't believe him.

'No,' said Jim. He put his ear close to his box. 'I can hear his motor running. It's a very quiet motor. Can you hear it?'

Jim's big sister stopped chewing her apple and listened. 'Are you sure that it's an engine I can hear, Jimbo? It's very quiet.'

'Sure it's an engine,' replied Jim. 'It's not very loud now because the robot is resting. I'll call you if he moves.'

Just before dinner, Jim began to open his box.

'Don't let your dragon out in my kitchen, Jim,' said his mother.

'Son, if that furry monster escapes, I'm going to the club,' said Jim's father.

'I'd like to see your robot, Jimbo,' said his sister, 'but I've got homework to do.'

'I'm just going to get him a bowl of milk,' said Jim.

'A robot that drinks milk!' exclaimed Jim's big sister.

'Didn't know furry monsters liked milk,' muttered his father.

'Do dragons drink milk?' asked his mother.

'Yes,' Jim told them all and put down the bowl of milk beside the box. 'You can come out now, your milk is ready.'

Jim turned to his mother, father and sister. 'Close your eyes, everyone, while I open the box.'

And they did.

'You mustn't even peep,' Jim said. Then he opened the box. 'You can open your eyes now!'

Jim's mother, father and sister opened their eyes.

'There's nothing there!' they all said at once.

'He decided that he didn't like milk after all, so he's gone home!' said Jim as he began to close the box.

'Was it a dragon?' asked Jim's mother.

'Or a furry monster?' asked Jim's father.

'Or a robot?' asked Jim's sister.

But Jim was off to the garden to collect some leaves so the box could become a new home for his snails.

Sock Eater

Jean Chapman

Hundred Legs had lots of socks, maybe thousands. Mostly they were long socks which he pulled up over his knees to keep them warm. He had red socks and green, blue socks and brown, grey, black and Argyle. He had socks with embroidered clocks on the sides. And striped socks, darned socks, old socks and holey socks but very few new socks. And *never ever* enough socks of matching kind and colour.

So, when the invitation came to Grasshopper's wedding, off he went to buy one hundred brand-new socks, one hundred, red-and-white-striped, long socks, all exactly alike.

'I'll wash them before I wear them,' he fussed, tearing the packages off the socks and tossing them into the washing machine.

Slish-slosh! The machine washed, swirling one hundred socks in froth and bubbles.

Whizz-whizz! It spun.

Swish-swirl! It rinsed.

Whizz-whizz! It spun.

Stretch-peg! Hundred Legs hung the socks on the line to dry.

On the wedding morning he started to pull on his freshly-washed, sun-dried, brand-new, red-and-white-striped, long socks. It took him a long time. All at once he had no more socks! and two of his feet were still bare!

No more socks! Hundred Legs was astonished.

Hadn't he bought one hundred socks, one for each foot? Yes, he had.

Had he or hadn't he put those one hundred, red-and-white-striped, long socks into the washing machine? Yes, he had.

Hadn't the machine washed them and rinsed them and spun them? Yes it had.

And hadn't he pegged them on the line to dry in the sun? Yes he had. Yes, *Yes!*

But . . . did he count the socks? *No!*

'I'll just have to have a sock hunt,' he said.

Hundred Legs looked in the washing machine. No socks there!

He looked in the garden and under the clothesline. No socks! He looked in drawers. He looked in cupboards and on the floors, under cushions and behind the doors. Under chairs and under the telly. In the oven and in the fridge. In the dustbin. Under the piano lid. In cake tins and saucepans, baskets and milk jugs, bottles and tins, and under every mat in the house. No socks! No socks were found. No newly-washed, sun-dried, red-and-white-striped, long socks. He found other things. Under his bed were two lost jumpers, an old apple core and lots of dust. There was plenty of fluff and heaps of dirty socks. In piles, raggy-taggy piles. And socks stuffed into the toes of old shoes.

'I'm still going to Grasshopper's wedding no matter what!' he said picking up two odd socks, a green and a blue. He put them on. Mmmm! His feet looked different. Rather smart, he thought. Hmmmm! He admired them in the mirror. At the same time he saw his red-and-white striped, long socks. 'Oh, no! No! No! *No!*' he wailed.

His brand new socks, the freshly washed, sun-dried, red-and-white-striped socks were dirty. Absolutely filthy! He had gone on his sock hunt without his shoes.

Off came the dirty socks. Into the washing machine. *Slosh-swish!* It started to wash and Hundred Legs humped off to make his bed which had four legs.

Slosh-slosh, chugga-chugga-chugga-ugga-ugga-ugg-ugg-clonk-ugg-clonk-onk-clonk! Bang! The washing machine stopped. Something smelt nasty and burnt. Hundred Legs rushed to the laundry. He turned off the machine. He bailed out the water and his socks. He wrung and he twisted and squeezed water from every one. He was too tired to count the socks as he slung them over the line to dry in the sun. And dry they were by wedding time.

One by one he put them on. It took a long time. Then there were no more socks left – again! Again! And Hundred Legs had more than two bare feet, more bare feet than he could count.

'Someone is pinching my socks!' he muttered. 'How can I go to the wedding now?'

He badly wanted to go. And he did. In bare feet.

It was a lovely wedding.

Next morning, not too early, he pulled the washing machine to pieces. He tapped and tinkered, screwed

and poked, pried and prodded, then pulled from its innards a long, skinny, slippery, greasy, red-and-whitish thing. Then another and another and another and another! What in the world were they?

Hundred Legs held one high. He looked at it in every way. He even smelt it. Then he yelled, 'So you're the dirty-sock eater!' And he gave the washing machine a good, hard thump.

It just stood there, just stood, of course. Later, it did wash Hundred Legs' socks again – and very clean they were – but it never ate another one.

Hundred Legs always carefully put his dirty socks into pillow slips before dropping them into the machine. So he still had one hundred, red-and-white-striped, long socks to wear to weddings and on other important occasions.

Acknowledgements

The compilers and publishers wish to thank the following for permission to use copyright material in this anthology.

The publishers have made every effort to trace copyright holders. If we have inadvertently omitted to acknowledge anyone we should be grateful if this could be brought to our attention for correction at the first opportunity.

Associated Book Publishers for 'Tumf' by W.J. Corbett from *The End of the Tale and Other Stories*

The Bodley Head for 'The Spider and the Prince' and 'Dribble's House' by Mies Bouheys from *The Paper Boat and Other Stories* and 'Lizard Comes Down from the North' by Anita Hewett from *The Anita Hewett Animal Story Book*

Howard Hoy for 'Aunt Emily's Pangolin' from *Helter Skelter* ed. P. Oldfield

Century Hutchinson for 'Mr Learn-a-Lot and the Singing Midges' by Alf Proysen from *Little Old Mrs Pepperpot*; 'Little Fly on the Ceiling' by Angela Pickering from *Animal Tales from Listen with Mother* and 'Wriggly Worm and Evil Weevil' by Eugenie Summerfield from *More Stories from Listen with Mother*

Jean Chapman for 'Sock Eater' from *Stories to Share* ed. Jean Chapman

Dent and Sons Ltd for 'The Insect Kingdom that didn't get Started' by Margaret Mahy from *Nonstop Nonsense*

Elaine for 'Grottie Germ and his Relations' from *Stories to Share* ed. Jean Chapman

Sarah Morcom for 'Reginald's Lousy Adventure' and 'Spider's Surprise'

Penguin Australia for 'The Elephant and the Beetle' by Patricia Adams and 'The Big Sore Toe' by Joanne Horniman from *Emu Stew* ed. Patricia Wrightson

Elizabeth Robinson for 'Big Spider Gets a Fright'